ZOMBIES

INVASION BRITAIN

ANTONY STEPHENS

ZOMBIES
INVASION BRITAIN

MEMOIRS
Cirencester

ALSO BY ANTONY STEPHENS:

Angela's Adventures in Rum-Tum Land (hardcover)
Book Guild Publishing, 2007
ISBN 978 1 84624 1789

Angela's Return to Rum-Tum Land (paperback)
Diadem Books, 2009
ISBN 978 1 90729 4238

Published by Memoirs

MEMOIRS
PUBLISHING

25 Market Place, Cirencester, Gloucestershire, GL7 2NX
info@memoirsbooks.co.uk www.memoirspublishing.com

ISBN: 978-1-909304-89-5

CHAPTER ONE

How did it come to this? thought Stephen Williams as he huddled amongst the evergreen and deciduous trees of Western Park shivering in the cold, unable even to light a fire for fear of alerting the zombies all around him to his whereabouts. *If only we had had some border controls, maybe they could have stopped the zombies.*

This was true enough for they had long since been abandoned with millions of people before the arrival of the zombies able to move freely across Europe.

Consequently in the year 2250 the population of Britain now numbered five hundred million. What had formerly been known as green-belt land had all been built on with the great national parks now concrete jungles; and the area of countryside that had surrounded the towns and cities comprising vast swathes of agricultural farmland had been bricked over as well, linking them with one another and forming megacities. Because there was no longer any farmland, crops could no longer be grown and so Britain had to import nearly its entire food supplies from abroad causing a huge trade deficit with the rest of the world. Town and city parks had come to be labelled green-belt land but not gardens and golf-courses that had been compulsorily purchased by many councils up and down the land to build more housing on.

The sole opposition to the government were fringe parties such as the greens who still argued in vain for the conservation of the remaining green-belt land and meaningful cuts in greenhouse gases before the planet boiled over. Temperatures had risen by two degrees over the centuries largely due to the continued use of non-eco-friendly fuels by countries such as the USA, India and China. The USA now had a population of one billion people and India and China each had ones that had grown to three billion people.

The population boom across the world and the increase in the gap between the wealth of the richest countries and that of the developing ones, had fuelled astronomical rises in illegal immigration with people desperate to escape the abject poverty in their home countries.

The historically unprecedented global population had helped to spread the zombie plague with more and more people living in such densely populated cities, often in close proximity to livestock which provided ideal conditions for novel diseases to emerge. And added to this the short time-lag between getting bitten and turning into a zombie yourself meant that the plague spread rapidly infecting entire cities in a matter of months.

The world's scientists had been working for almost a year to try to find a cure for it without success. Not that this mattered much anymore to Stephen Williams for he had lost his parents, his wife and two daughters. And now he was all alone rueing the destruction of his once great country. *But the zombies will not get me without a fight*! he thought as he continued to walk past the bushes in the park where they were hidden like mindless automata with blank staring eyes, congealed blood around their mouths and bits of rotting flesh hanging off their bodies.

He vowed that he was going to destroy as many of them as he could with his trusty Browning 9mm pistol which had been in service since WWII and had proven itself to be a reliable, accurate and robust weapon with an effective range of up to 45 metres. He had managed to grab loads of magazines for it each with a capacity of thirteen rounds which he had stuffed into all his jacket and trouser pockets, and he was grateful at least that the sale of hand-guns had been legalised decades before because of the soaring violence.

Stephen had already killed numerous zombies by shooting them through the head which he knew was the only way to kill them as it was only when the brain died that their bodies did as well. As he watched them walk relentlessly past him searching out more victims impervious to pain, fear or reason he pointed his gun ahead of him, ready to shoot his way out of the park if necessary.

Eventually and to Stephen's relief there were no more zombies to be seen and he took a rucksack off his back, and then opened a tin of beans with a can-opener from his Swiss-army knife. He then ate the beans all the while listening out for the rustling of leaves or twigs snapping underfoot for he knew that the zombies could be lucky and stumble upon him.

After consuming the beans he tossed the can aside, took out a sleeping-bag from his rucksack and unfurled it on the ground. Then climbing inside it he closed his eyes and went to sleep. After a while his eyes were moving rapidly as he dreamed of the time he and his wife Rosie had taken their two daughters, Allison and Samantha, to pick strawberries. They had beamed in delight on seeing the succulent fruit and had bounded between the aisles where their plants had been stacked in grow-bags on raised platforms, alternately putting them in their punnets and popping them in their mouths.

Suddenly Stephen was roused from his slumber by a rattling noise emanating from a trip-wire he had set up between two trees with tin cans attached to it. A zombie had walked into it and was now bearing down on him, his arms held out in front of him while emitting a groaning dirge. In an instant Stephen reached for the pistol lying on the end of his sleeping-bag and fired one shot from it at the zombie hitting him right between his temples, whereupon he fell down dead on top of him.

'Ugh! Get off me!' said Stephen shoving the lifeless creature away from him.

At that moment he heard a succession of horrible groans as more zombies made their way towards him. Quickly he rolled up his sleeping-bag and placed it in his rucksack which he then slung over his back.

'I'm not wasting,' he said, 'any more bullets on you fuckers!'

With that he ran through the trees away from the zombies who fortunately for him could only move very slowly. Nevertheless it had not stopped them cornering and killing thousands of people for they were so vast in number, and were relentless in pursuit of their victims, eager to devour their flesh.

Stephen moved quickly and stealthily through the park past the old 19ᵗʰ century pavilion incorporating a café, and on past a bandstand and a majestic fountain resplendent with four bronze lions out of whose mouths water was shooting into the air. He shuddered as he thought of all the people he had seen being eaten alive whom he had been powerless to help: innocent men, women and children.

The land forming the boundary with Western Park was a high rocky ridge which had once allowed delightful views of the open countryside beyond but was now full of houses and factories. The park comprised different levels to the front and rear and Stephen stealthily made his way through its terraced gardens which swept down it.

At the edge of the trees he paused momentarily before running out onto a road lined with houses in the Arts and Crafts style built from local materials and which had once perfectly fitted into the landscape. The way was illuminated by street-lamps that flickered on and off and he felt exposed running along the road. He had never been more grateful that he had a gun on him which his friends had chastised him for getting, telling him that he was unlikely to ever need it as he and his family lived in a nice area that was relatively crime free.

How wrong they had been for the march of the zombies had made people desperate for something to eat who had begun to ransack houses in search of food; and Stephen had been forced to kill a couple of intruders to protect his family's supplies which they had stored in the cellar, for the supplies were limited and he could not have afforded to have given any of it away. To him his wife and daughters came first and that had been his motto until the day they had died.

CHAPTER TWO

Stephen ran past the upturned cars and ones that had crashed into shop-front windows as their desperate owners had tried to drive away from the zombies, who had leapt onto their cars en masse and broken their windscreens and windows with rocks and metal poles. Most vehicles did not look in any condition to drive and in any case the zombies had removed the keys that had still been left in the ignitions preventing people from using them to get away—that is, the ones who did not know how to hot-wire them.

On rare occasions Stephen had successfully inserted a slotted screwdriver in the ignition and turned it over like a regular key or failing this had managed to hot-wire them, although he was extremely reluctant to attempt this as it was a very tricky procedure that could result in receiving painful electric shocks. To begin with he had always been forced to remove the large plastic panels that snapped together and covered the top and bottom of the steering column, so that the cylinder and the wires running into it were exposed.

After he had done this he would be faced with three pairs of wires running into the back of the cylinder—each pair representing a different key position on the ignition. One pair would trigger the battery-only position, another the lights and radio position and one pair was responsible for the final key position—starting the car. Unfortunately there was no universal colour system for the wires and if you didn't have access to the relevant car's manual you could not find out its specific colour code. However the red pair was normally the set that provided power to the car and the brown handled the starter.

Once Stephen had located the wires that provided power to the car he would disconnect them from the cylinder using his wire stripper to remove the plastic from the ends and then would twist them together, knowing he was successful if there was power to the dashboard, lights and just about everything else in the car. It was then things got dangerous for the wires responsible for starting the car carried live current, and when he had stripped the insulation off the ends of them he was extremely careful not to handle the exposed parts as he touched them together. If all had gone to plan he would hear a spark and the engine fire up whereupon once it was idling he would separate and cover the ends of the starter wires.

Stephen had only been successful on a few occasions in hot-wiring cars, for even when he had managed to get them started the vast majority of them had a mechanism that locked the steering wheel unless a key was in the ignition so that he had simply been unable to turn it. Naturally enough his poor success rate and the time and effort plus the hazards of electrical shocks involved in hot-wiring cars had made him extremely reluctant to attempt to do so. Instead he preferred to walk everywhere occasionally checking cars to see if keys had been left in their ignition whereupon he would attempt to start them, although on the odd occasions this had happened the car's battery had invariably turned out to be flat and the engine would not turn over.

For now though Stephen had to think of what he was going to do next as he made his way through the city negotiating the deserted ring roads, bus lanes and one-way systems, passing the textile factories that had had all their windows smashed in by the workers there. They had leapt to the ground to evade the zombies sometimes to their deaths from the upper floors, but more often than not sustaining broken legs and ankles in the process thereby rendering them incapable of getting away and being eaten alive.

At the end of a road Stephen turned left into another which seemed to be clear, the only thing visible being a buzzing neon sign with *café* written on it. However he had got about half way across it when some zombies appeared out of a side-street and made for him. He was about to run back the way he had come when he saw another group of zombies at the other end of the road. *Shit! I'm cut off!* he thought.

Trying to figure out what to do next he looked around and noticed an alleyway going round the back of a red-brick factory with an imposing clock tower and he ran down it. To his horror he found it did not lead anywhere but was just a dead-end.

'Fucking hell!' he said. 'I don't have a lot of options now!'

Stephen tried several doors and found one open that led into the factory and was about to go into it when he realised the zombies would follow behind him and corner him there. All the time they were closing in on him as he paced around wondering what to do next.

He was alerted when they had reached the alleyway by a series of groans and he looked to the other end of it to see them shuffling towards him, their eyes staring horribly at him out of their decaying heads.

'Oh fuck! I've had it!' said Stephen. 'But at least I'll take a few of these bastards with me!'

So saying he fired thirteen shots wounding five and killing eight of them. The injured kept on coming with the others however for it did not matter how many times they were shot in their body, only a bullet to the head could down them. Discarding his gun's empty magazine Stephen put a new one into it and fired off a few more rounds killing another two of them before spotting a ladder in one corner of the alleyway that went up to the roof.

'I just might get out of this yet!' he exclaimed.

He darted over to the ladder and began to climb it but did not get far before his left leg was grabbed from behind. Like lightning Stephen swivelled round and fired at point-blank range at a zombie who slumped back down on the ground. In a minute Stephen had reached the top of the ladder and stepped off it onto the factory-roof, from where he took a few more pot-shots at the zombies who had started to climb up the ladder after him making them fall off it and land in a pile on the ground.

'It took me almost one and a half magazines,' he said, 'to get out of that! I can't afford to keep on getting through ammo at that rate!'

He hurried across the roof until he came to the edge of it where there was a considerable gap between it and the roof of the adjacent factory.

'I'm going to have to jump this gap,' said Stephen who had developed a habit of talking to himself for it had been so long since he had had human companionship.

Taking about thirty steps backwards he breathed in deeply and then ran towards the edge of the roof, propelling himself off it, clearing the gap and the large drop to the ground and landing safely on the opposite roof.

'Made it!' he said in relief straightening himself up.

Stephen ran across the roof dodging the air vents and chimneys, pausing momentarily to peer down through a skylight to see upturned sewing-machines and tables strewn across the floor, where the zombies had rampaged through the factory. Up above a full moon shone its blue light on him as he jumped from roof to roof like a cat-burglar until he came to the final building at the end of the road where he climbed down a ladder and set foot in another alleyway.

Walking slowly to the end of it he turned round in fright when he heard the sound of crying and was relieved to see it was just a stray cat searching for food amongst some bins. At the end of the alleyway he glanced down both sides of the road it bordered before setting off down it, ducking down behind abandoned cars whenever he thought he heard a noise.

As Stephen came upon shops he always stopped to check if they had any food in them. However they had been ransacked long ago. It was an eerie feeling as he passed all the deserted offices and factories where once people had worked. He glanced at his watch. It was two o'clock in the morning but the zombies never got tired or slept so he was lucky if he could get a few hours' sleep every night himself.

At the end of the street he ran across a road to a roundabout where he concealed himself amongst some overgrown bushes before some zombies heading his way could see him. He had to wait some time for them to go past whereupon he got to his feet. The street he now followed led on to an underpass which took him beneath a bridge whose support pillars were beginning to crack and crumble, and he thought it would not be much longer before it totally collapsed. He passed a succession of roundabouts which along with parks, gardens, allotments, trees, plant containers and hanging baskets still made Leicester a very green city. They had provided an oasis within the bustle of shops, houses and traffic with even some of the public libraries boasting lawns complete with flowerbeds as you approached their entrances.

Stephen was running low on food so he decided to check out all the supermarkets which he knew were still practically stocked full of tinned goods. Sticking to the side-streets where he thought he'd be safer he went past the red-bricked court-building, and then turned left by a multi-storey car-park and proceeded onwards up a slight hill. At the top of it he glanced round a wall to see two zombies coming towards him.

'Sod it!' said Stephen. 'That's the direction I need to go and I can't afford to hang around here for those two living dead to go by!'

So saying he broke cover and walked nonchalantly towards them shooting them both in the head and then stepping over their lifeless bodies. He went by a succession of abandoned cars for quite a distance before he thought he saw something move from behind a Volkswagen Beetle to a Citroen and duck down there.

'Oh great!' he said. 'Another one of them!'

Naturally enough he had assumed what he had seen had been a zombie and paced towards the parked Citroen ready to despatch it. When he was near to the car and preparing to go round the back of it a little girl wearing boots, jeans and a duffel-coat suddenly broke cover and attempted to run away.

Stephen aimed his gun and fired at her but just at that moment she happened to trip and the bullet whizzed over her head.

'No, don't shoot!' she said. 'I'm not a zombie! I'm human!'

'Put your hands,' said Stephen, 'on your head and come here so I can have a better look at you.'

The little girl did as he said, got to her feet and walked slowly towards him. Examining her intently he saw that her face and clothes were covered in dirt but other than that there appeared to be no signs of putrefaction on her body.

'Shit! You *are* human!' said Stephen, 'and I nearly fucking killed you! You should have said before!'

'You didn't give me the chance!' said the girl.

'I just killed,' said Stephen, 'two zombies before I saw you. They made me rather jumpy.'

'I'll say!' said the girl. 'Can I take my hands off my head now?'

Stephen's face went red with embarrassment and he said, 'Yes, of course. What's your name?'

'Julie Mayberry,' said the girl.

'And I'm Stephen Williams,' said Stephen. 'I had a couple of daughters, Allison and Samantha but they were both killed by the zombies. Allison was twelve and Samantha eleven. She was just like you with long blonde hair and hazel eyes. How old are you?'

'Nine,' said Julie.

Stephen's eyes momentarily glazed over as he visualised his daughters standing in front of him before his attention turned to Julie once again.

'Are your parents still alive?' he said.

'No,' said Julie. 'They were killed a few months ago by the zombies.'

She began to cry and Stephen removed a tissue from his rucksack, gave it to her and placed his hand on her shoulder to try to comfort her.

'How have you managed,' he said, 'to survive on your own in the meantime?'

'I've been going,' said Julie wiping her eyes with the tissue, 'to the supermarket every couple of days to get food and been sleeping on the beds they have on display in department stores at night.'

'That's a risky business,' said Stephen. 'The zombies could easily corner you in them.'

'I've always,' said Julie, 'managed to hide from them when I've spotted them.'

'So far,' said Stephen, 'but your luck will run out sooner or later. You'd be better off sleeping out in the open like me.'

'But it's so cold at night,' said Julie.

As if in emphasis of this point she did up another toggle on her duffel-coat and shivered violently.

'D'you want to come with me?' said Stephen. 'I'm off to the supermarket to get some food.'

'Yes,' said Julie. 'I was on my way there when I saw you.'

'I think,' said Stephen, 'we should get you a rucksack and a sleeping-bag as well so that you can sleep out in the open if need be.'

With that the two of them headed off to the supermarket.

CHAPTER THREE

The city of Leicester Stephen and Julie were in had once been a teeming chaotic expanse with overcrowded streets bursting with life and vigour and a suburban sprawl with terraced houses, villas, tower blocks, churches and cinemas which were now all deserted. They walked past a book-shop which Stephen regularly visited who had become an avid reader for it had helped to alleviate the boredom of being on his own all the time.

'Have you read,' he said to Julie, 'as they stopped by the window, 'Alice In Wonderland or Peter Pan yet?'

'Yes,' she said, 'or rather my mother read them to me. I thought they were great.'

'Well,' said Stephen, 'we could go in the book-shop and pick up some books that I could read to you if you want?'

'Yes,' said Julie. 'I'd like that very much.'

So they entered the shop and made their way to the

children's books section where Stephen picked out copies of A little Princess, The Secret Garden, Treasure Island, The Wizard Of Oz, The Wind In The Willows, Watership Down, Harry Potter And The Philosopher's Stone and Northern Lights.

'That,' he said, 'should be enough to be going on with.'

He stuffed the books into his rucksack and the two of them headed towards the door but before they reached it they heard a noise, and they turned to their right to see a zombie walking down the steps leading to the second floor with a horrible wide-eyed vacant look on her face.

'Close your eyes,' said Stephen, 'and cover your ears Julie!'

She did as ordered at which point Stephen shot the zombie who fell over and rolled the rest of the way down the stairs.

'It's alright now,' said Stephen ushering Julie out of the shop.

After going through the door they turned right and carried on through a pedestrian-zone until they came to an alleyway which led out onto a large market where rotten fruit and vegetables were on the shelves. It was bordered by a row of shops mainly selling books and electrical goods which they ignored. Soon they came upon another alleyway and went down it to the main shopping-zone in town. It was where all the big department stores were, many of which served tinned food on their ground floors. This was important as it preserved it and ensured that it was fresh unlike things such as bread, cheese and sliced meat in plastic packaging that had long ago gone mouldy.

Stephen collected a shopping-trolley and he and Julie proceeded up and down the aisles pausing to put any cans of food they could find in their basket. When it was full up with baked beans, spaghetti hoops, macaroni cheese, ravioli and frankfurters they made their way to the till, where they transferred all their goods from their trolley onto it and then into Stephen's rucksack.

'At least,' he laughed, 'there's one good thing about the zombies: we no longer need to pay for all this.'

Julie smiled as they walked out of the shop and headed for the camping-store directly opposite. Inside it they picked out a rucksack, sleeping-bag and a Swiss-army knife for her plus a two-person tent. On exiting the shop they looked to their right and left. There were a group of zombies but they were some way up the road on their left-hand side.

Relieved, they sprinted across the road to the opposite pavement and continued onwards to a bridge which passed over a river on which they caught a glimpse of silver sunlight as it snaked between the grey buildings.

'I've got,' said Stephen, 'to get some more ammo for my gun. Without it we're done for.'

'D'you know where we can get it?' said Julie.

'Yes, a gun-shop,' said Stephen. 'That's where we're off to now. Let's hope we don't encounter any zombies before then.'

'I can't believe,' said Julie, 'how many of them you've killed already. Where did you learn how to shoot like that?'

Stephen smiled and said, 'At a gun-range when I was in the RAF. I'm glad I put in many hours of practice firing at targets. It means I'm able to hit something from quite far away. It's saved my life on many occasions.'

'And mine,' said Julie.

'I'm glad to help,' said Stephen. 'It's nice to have someone to talk to apart from myself all day.'

This was indeed true despite the fact that Julie was only nine years old for she was still a member of the human race and reminded Stephen he was too. They carried on along a tree-lined road whose branches were swaying in a light breeze. They were the only ones on it for as far as the eye could see as they walked past the empty houses which gave the road an eerie feel as though they had entered a ghost-town. They passed an old pub with a walled beer-garden whose stained-glass windows had been smashed in as zombies had rampaged through it. In the distance, framed by the trees, the tops of blocks of flats could be seen.

On Stephen and Julie went along a little street of small shops and sandwich bars, spotting one of a series of manhole covers that had been removed as people desperately tried to escape from the zombies into the sewers and their network of tunnels that honeycombed through the cold clay beneath the city's streets. The next road they came to had a terrace of houses all with balconies at first-floor level which was interjected with streets of bijou residences in exclusive residential districts.

Suddenly Stephen became alert as he spotted a sign with *Green Park* written on it and said, 'That's the shopping-centre where I bought my ammunition for my Browning 9mm gun. However I had a car then and didn't have to walk all this way.'

'How far away is it?' said Julie yawning.

'About five miles,' said Stephen.

The route led on through council estates and along roads lined with speed-cameras; and Stephen thought it ironic that they and all the CCTV cameras everywhere that had been supposed to increase security and lessen fatalities on the roads and in the cities, had not been able to do anything to halt the advance of the zombies. In frustration he stuck two fingers up to one, half wishing that the pictures it was receiving were being relayed to a normal human being somewhere.

Whenever he and Julie spotted zombies up ahead of them they would duck down side streets until they had passed before continuing on their way. After a while they came to a roundabout around which cars had stopped bumper to bumper, and their occupants had fought desperate battles with the zombies to try to save their lives. Some people had been armed and had managed to kill several zombies before running out of bullets and being disembowelled by them, for they had not had the chance to stock up on ammunition like Stephen had had.

He and Julie went straight on at the roundabout passing a pub, then beneath a bridge and on past a rubbish-tip, where a few stray dogs were scavenging amongst the discarded black refuse-bags. They gave Stephen the creeps for he had had to shoot a few before that had been bitten by zombies and turned into ones themselves. And if you can imagine this happening to Pit Bulls, Dobermans and Alsatians who were terrifying enough anyway, then you would have known the kind of fear Stephen had felt when he had been confronted by them.

So he and Julie hurried past the dump knowing there was no way they could outrun the dogs if they should happen to spot them and give chase. Stephen had even heard of some that had not been turned into zombies who nevertheless had been so crazed with hunger that they had attacked and eaten humans anyway.

They came upon another sign with Green Park on it and an arrow below it pointing to their right, an ironic name Stephen thought as it was comprised entirely of concrete as was most of the rest of Britain. Crossing the road they turned right at another sign and entered the shopping-complex.

CHAPTER FOUR

Stephen and Julie walked through the large car-park of the shopping-centre keeping a watchful eye out for zombies. None seemed to be around and so they headed for the gun-shop which was next to a supermarket, an odd juxtaposition you might think but not in the new Britain.

When they had reached the gun-store where various rifles and pistols were displayed in the window Stephen ducked down, pushing Julie down with him for there were five zombies in the store.

'Fucking great!' said Stephen. 'Now we can't get to the ammo with those zombies there!'

'I know!' said Julie. 'I can lure them out and then you can go and get some!'

'That'd be very dangerous,' said Stephen. 'I'm not sure I like that idea.'

'Look,' said Julie, 'we've come all this way and if we don't get some more ammunition we're dead anyway, aren't we?'

'Okay then,' said Stephen. 'We'll do it your way. I'll hide behind a car and you lead the zombies away from the shopping-centre.'

He quickly went and concealed himself behind one of the many parked cars in the car-park which resembled a graveyard for them as they remained unclaimed by their owners who had long since died. When he had done so Julie opened the gun-shop door and said, 'Hey zombies! Over here!' They all turned to face her and shuffled towards her as she waited by the door.

'I wish,' said Stephen, 'at times like this those creatures could move a bit faster.'

He remained where he was as the zombies exited the gun-shop and followed Julie who led them out of the car-park like a bizarre Pied Piper of Hamlin. When finally they were all out of view Stephen rushed over to the gun-shop where he managed to find about a dozen replacement magazines for his gun which he stuffed into his rucksack. He also picked out a crossbow and a quiver full of ten arrows thinking that Julie might feel more comfortable handling it than a gun.

When he had got what he needed he was about to leave the shop when he spotted a gun-holster whereupon he immediately took his brown jacket off, and strapped it over his left shoulder before putting his jacket back on again. He then left the shop, hid behind another car and waited for the little girl he was growing to be quite fond of to return.

After an hour had gone by he was just beginning to get worried about her when to his joy he spotted her running into the car-park. He immediately got to his feet and went to meet her.

'How did you get on?' he said to her.

'I got the zombies,' she said, 'to follow me down a long road and when I had turned a corner and they could not see me, I climbed a wall and hid in a garden. Then when they had gone past me I doubled back and returned here.'

'You did well,' said Stephen smiling and he could not have been more proud of her than if she had been his own daughter. 'Here, I got this for you. Take it.'

He handed her the crossbow and the quiver full of arrows, the latter of which she slung over her back.

'Right, I'll show you how to load it,' said Stephen as Julie watched him intently. 'First you draw back the bow string then place an arrow in front of it on the stick like this, then you line up your target until you can see it in the crosshairs of your telescopic sight at which point you're ready to fire. D'you think you'll be able to remember all that?'

'Yes,' said Julie. 'I've done a bit of archery before at school but I was shooting at a target then, not a real person.'

'The zombies,' said Stephen, 'are not *real* people. Just you remember that.'

Julie nodded as they both headed into the supermarket next door to the gun-shop where they walked up and down the aisles that were completely deserted stocking up on food and water.

'It's like a ghost-town around here,' said Julie. 'I can't remember when I last saw a normal human being, apart from you that is of course.'

'Nor me,' said Stephen taking a swig from a bottle of mineral water before passing it to Julie who did likewise. 'There's not even any countryside for us to escape to anymore. I always wanted to live in the country when I was young but the remaining parts of it were eaten up in yours and my lifetime. Now future generations will never again be able to see green fields and wild flowers again.'

When they had got what they needed they left the supermarket to be greeted by the five zombies that Julie had led away from the gun-shop some time previously, like homing pigeons returning to their coup.

Stephen nonchalantly removed his gun from its new holster and fired four bullets into the heads of four of the zombies who toppled onto the ground like he was shooting cans off a wall.

'There's still one left,' said Julie. 'Why haven't you shot it?'

'I've left it for you,' said Stephen. 'It'll be good target practise.'

'I don't know,' said Julie, 'if I can kill it.'

'You've got to,' said Stephen. 'It'll help to save your life one day. I might not always be around to do so.'

'Don't say that,' said Julie. 'I don't want to be left on my own again.'

'There's less chance,' said Stephen, 'of that happening if you can cover my back like I'm covering yours. C'mon, I'll show you what to do again. Right, you look through the crossbow's telescopic sight like this and when your target is in the crosshairs gently squeeze the trigger.'

Stephen stood round the back of Julie taking it in turns to peer through the crossbow's sight with her manoeuvring her arms so that she was pointing it right at the zombie's head who had advanced to within twenty yards of them.

'That looks about right,' said Stephen. 'Now fire!'

Julie pressed the trigger of the crossbow and the arrow was released and the next instant it lodged in the zombie's neck, who did not even flinch as he continued towards them.

'Not bad,' said Stephen, 'for a first attempt. Get another arrow and reload the crossbow.'

Julie's hands trembled as she reached for one from the quiver slung across her back all the time keeping one eye on the zombie whose contorted green and purple face looked quite disgusting. Drawing back the bow string until it was held firmly in place by a mechanism on the stock she placed the arrow on it, and then aimed the crossbow once again with Stephen's help before firing it. This time the arrow flew into the zombie's head and penetrated its brain causing it to drop stone dead.

'You did it!' said Stephen applauding as he walked up to it, pulled the two arrows from its body which he wiped clean with a rag before he handed them to Julie who winced as she put them back in her quiver. 'You see, only after a couple of tries you're producing shots with the deadly accuracy of a true professional! And now you've killed your first zombie it should be far easier from now on.'

Tears streamed down Julie's eyes as she said, 'I don't know if I want to kill any others.'

'I'm afraid,' said Stephen, 'you might have to if you and me are both to survive. C'mon, let's get out of here. You'll feel better later on, you'll see.'

Julie was not altogether convinced by this as she loaded another arrow automatically into her crossbow and put her rucksack back on. She and Stephen then left the shopping-centre through the car-park and walked back the way they had come onto the main road.

'H'm,' said Stephen as they halted in their tracks momentarily, 'we should leave Leicester behind and go on to Nottingham. Who knows? We may find normal human beings like ourselves there.'

Due to the building on all the Green-Belt land surrounding Leicester, Nottingham, Coventry, Derby, Stoke and Birmingham they had merged with one another and had become a megacity, with only commons separating them so that they could still be distinguished from one another.

Stephen and Julie walked through an ancient thoroughfare where there were many large houses with black spiked gates and long driveways leading up to them. They proceeded to a junction where they turned right and by this time the light had begun to darken and Stephen said, 'We'll have to look for somewhere to shelter. It'll be night time soon.'

They continued on for quite some distance down a sloping road lined with a majestic row of elm trees before they came upon a double-decker bus still parked beside a bus stop.

'This'll,' said Stephen, 'be a good place to spend the night—on the top deck of this bus.'

'I thought,' said Julie, 'you said it was much safer to sleep out in the open?'

'It is ordinarily,' said Stephen, 'but I can't see any zombies around and in any case I feel too tired to put our tent up what with all the walking we've done today.'

So the two of them entered the bus through the doors which had fortunately been left open.

'Good!' said Stephen checking the driver's cab. 'The keys are still in the ignition.'

With that they went up to the top deck where they removed their rucksacks and slung them down on some seats.

'Let's have something to eat now,' said Stephen sitting down on one of the front seats, as did Julie.

He took out two tins of ravioli from his rucksack, opened them both and handed one to Julie. Then they tucked into them as they looked out at the road stretching out before them which continued for some way downhill before sloping upwards.

By the time they had finished their ravioli which they washed down with some mineral water, a full moon had appeared in the sky casting a silver beam of light over the surrounding area.

'Would you like me to read you a story, Julie?' said Stephen.

'Yes please,' she beamed.

'Okay then,' said Stephen looking through the books they had got in the library a couple of days before. 'I think we'll start with A Little Princess by Frances Hodgson Burnett.'

He removed a torch from his rucksack, switched it on and then turned to chapter one of the book

CHAPTER FIVE

The following morning Stephen and Julie awoke after a fairly good night's sleep on the top deck of the double-decker bus, yawned and stretched themselves. Stephen straightened his brown hair, rubbed his bleary green eyes and looked out on the road in front of them.

'Fucking hell!' he said. 'There are zombies everywhere!'

There were about thirty who had congregated in the middle of the road and who were marching in unison towards the bus like some robotic army.

'Check the back of the bus, Julie!' said Stephen continuing to keep watch on the progress of the zombies at the front of it.

Julie hurried to the back of the bus and looked out the window to see to her horror about twenty more zombies heading their way from that end also.

'There's loads this side as well!' she said. 'We're trapped!'

'Maybe not!' said Stephen. 'I've got an idea!'

He rushed downstairs with Julie following behind him, got into the driver's cab and turned the keys into the ignition. To his horror there was no response from the engine and he banged the steering-wheel in frustration with both hands and shouted out, 'Start! Fucking start!'

After several more goes the engine finally spluttered into life whereupon the bus began to move forward before the engine conked out again.

'Oh no!' said Julie as the zombie-army bore down on them from both sides of the bus. 'The engine's stopped running!'

'No matter,' said Stephen. 'The bus is moving but I can't get the doors to close. They seem to be jammed.'

Gradually it built up momentum as it freewheeled towards the zombies still walking dementedly on towards it.

'C'mon, c'mon!' said Stephen. 'We need more speed!'

The bus duly obliged as though it was a sentient being that could hear him and sped towards the zombies.

'Right, here goes!' said Stephen. 'Get ready for impact!'

Julie clung onto a hand-rail as the bus collided with the zombies crushing them beneath it one after the other like ants as it ploughed through them.

'Fucking great! Fucking great!' said Stephen.

By now some of the zombies had veered away from the main group and as the bus passed by them they attempted to climb into it. However before they could do so Julie had fired arrows at them with her crossbow and they fell backwards onto the road.

The bus continued right to the bottom of the hill and then went up another slope a little way before rolling backwards again, having killed all of the zombies that had been in the way of it, leaving twenty zombies still alive who had been following behind the bus all this time.

'Let's get out of here!' said Stephen to Julie as he clambered out of the driver's seat and then they both jumped down from the still moving bus, before running up the hill away from the remaining zombies who were some way behind.

On reaching the top of the hill Stephen turned round and shouted down to them, 'We beat you, you bastards, like we'll always beat you if you don't leave us alone!' This was just a show of bravado for deep down in his heart he did not really believe that, but he had become so protective of Julie by now that he could not bear to think of the zombies getting their horrible decaying hands on her.

They turned round and carried on with their journey not really knowing where it would take them, but hoping that they would somehow find a refuge in the concrete jungle where they could find peace. As they walked along they paused by each side street and looked down it to make sure no zombies were lurking there. It had been a couple of days since they had met up but still they had encountered no other human beings.

At about midday after passing through a once busy shopping area with a number of specialist shops together with a cosmopolitan spread of restaurants and a pub, they turned into a park through its open black wrought-iron gates and walked through it until they came to a bench by a duck-pond. They sat down on it and watched the ducks paddling around on the pond, some of whom swam right up to the bank near to them and quacked plaintively hoping to receive some bread.

Stephen and Julie did not have any to give them though for all the loaves in the shops and supermarkets had gone mouldy being well past their sell-by-date. They took pleasure in their tranquil, green surroundings and would have gladly set up home there if it had not been for the zombies.

'It's so nice,' said Stephen, 'to be away from the zombies even for a few moments. There aren't many places like this where you can see so much greenery.'

'I know,' said Julie, 'but my grandparents told me there had still been great national parks in their day.'

'We've lost them forever,' said Stephen.

They got to their feet and proceeded the rest of the way through the park admiring the profusion of golden daffodils in the flower-beds. On exiting the park they came out onto a street lined with trees whose overhanging branches formed an arch across it and which had almost all been colonised by grey squirrels, who had driven the remaining pockets of red squirrels into extinction some years before.

It was late afternoon by the time they reached the outskirts of Nottingham and found themselves standing at the top of a hill overlooking a sloping road that led for a long way downwards. They were just beginning to think they would have to walk all the way down it when Julie saw a bicycle lying in one of the driveways and said, 'Maybe we can use that?'

'Good thinking!' said Stephen. 'My legs are starting to ache.'

'So are mine,' said Julie.

Stephen went over to the bike, pulled it up off the ground and wheeled it over to Julie. After straddling it he said to her, 'You sit on the back of the saddle—oh, and you better take this.' He took his pistol out of his pocket and handed it to her along with a couple of magazines.

'I don't know how to use it,' said Julie.

'It's easy,' said Stephen releasing the safety-catch. 'You just point it at your target and squeeze the trigger. There are thirteen rounds to a magazine and when you've emptied it simply withdraw it from the butt of the gun like this,' here he showed her how to do it, 'and then load another one into it like this. Got it?'

'Yes, I think so,' said Julie.

'Good,' said Stephen. 'We can be off then. If you see any zombies drop them.'

He pushed off with the bicycle and they began to

freewheel down the hill. All seemed to be going well when all of a sudden, one by one, doors opened and zombies began to emerge from all the houses lining the road. *Suburban hell*! thought Stephen who then called out, 'Get ready Julie. It looks like we've got company!' He began to peddle the bike in order to go faster to try to evade the zombies but it was a long road, and by the time they were half way down it a lot of them had exited the garden-gates and had stepped into the road.

Julie opened fire from side to side missing with her first few shots until she found her aim, and then there was no stopping her as the bullets from her gun smashed into the zombies' heads showering the road with bits of their brains and skulls. She only stopped firing to reload her gun before the bangs could be heard again. At the end of the road she and Stephen turned a corner and left the zombies behind.

'You did great Julie!' said Stephen beaming. 'I couldn't have done better myself!'

'I've used up,' she said, 'all the magazines you gave me in the process though.'

'Don't worry about it,' said Stephen. 'I've still got plenty left plus you've got your crossbow as well.'

As the road they were now on was flat they were unable to freewheel any longer and Stephen was forced to peddle the bike along it puffing and panting as he did so. They did see the occasional zombie as they went along but too far away to do them any damage.

They passed by all kinds of houses and through areas where once there had been over a century of architectural history to be found from mid-Victorian solidity to elegant Arts and Crafts particularly in the Edwardian period. Only a few of the original houses still existed with blocks of flats having infiltrated the areas which were struggling to still exude leafy middle-class suburbia.

Stephen was beginning to tire and thinking of stopping when he saw a sign up ahead of him which said Bramley Airport. Bramley had been a small village on the outskirts of Nottingham surrounded by countryside but which had merged with the city because of the never ending house-building programme instituted by the government.

Thinking it would be a good place to stop for the night Stephen turned into it, and rode himself and Julie along a narrow, winding road past a café, go-kart track and then a large hanger in which there were two Cessna 152's, a Piper PA28-161 Cadet and a Slingsby T67m Firefly. On emerging round a corner they saw a few white-walled buildings and a control tower as well as two more hangers not far from some fuel pumps in which there were more light aircraft.

In front of the control tower were two secondary runways intersecting a third main runway in a triangular formation, which were blocked by a Piper PA28R Arrow III and a Grob G115 that had been stopped from taking off when the zombies had overrun the airport and killed all the pilots and passengers on them.

Stephen rode the bicycle up to the control-tower where he brought it to a halt, and then he and Julie walked up some steps to it and went through a door. On the other side of it was a reception-area where once staff had been on duty seven days a week 365 days a year. After checking out the ground floor they went up a flight of steps which led to a lounge clubroom and bar and at the top of the steps was the control tower itself.

Returning to the lounge they walked out onto a comfortable and warm covered viewing balcony.

'The view's great from here, isn't it?' said Stephen.

'Yes, it is,' said Julie. 'It must have been fun to fly planes from here.'

'Yes, I've flown a few myself,' said Stephen. 'Helicopters were my thing though. I told you didn't I that I used to be in the RAF but I left ten years ago? That's where I first learnt how to use a Browning 9mm pistol. The RAF regiment uses it as a secondary weapon whilst on patrol and as a primary weapon where space is restricted like on diving duties.'

'Why did you leave the RAF?' said Julie sitting down on a chair.

Stephen sat down on one beside her and said, 'Well, I flew choppers in the third Falklands war against the Argentinians ferrying supplies from ship to shore and I was shot down by an enemy fighter-jet, which killed my co-pilot but luckily I survived if you can call it that. When we won the war and returned back home I began to suffer from post-traumatic stress disorder and was forced to leave the air force. I haven't flown since.'

He was silent for a moment before saying to Julie, 'Can I have my gun back now? I think I'll give it a good clean.'

She gave it to him and watched in admiration as he dismantled it and began to clean it with some oil and a rag before reassembling it again.

'I learnt,' he said, 'to do that in the RAF as well. We chopper pilots always carried a pistol on us in case we got shot down. We learnt how important it is to keep them clean to prevent them from jamming and we wouldn't want that to happen with thousand upon thousand of zombies around, would we?'

By now they were both feeling very hungry as they had not had anything to eat since breakfast because they had to ration their food, so they were forced to have a drink of water each instead to try to stop their stomachs from rumbling. Then Stephen read some more of the story of Sara Crewe to Julie from A Little Princess before they got into their sleeping-bags and closed their eyes.

CHAPTER SIX

Stephen and Julie were awoken by bright sunlight streaming in through the windows of the lounge at the airport and they both clambered out of their sleeping-bags, got to their feet and walked out onto the viewing balcony once more.

'Aargh!' screamed Julie as she and Stephen saw about a hundred zombies moving towards them.

'Shit!' said Stephen. 'We never have a moment's rest from those monsters!'

He and Julie packed their things away, exited the lounge and ran down the stairs and out of the building. Stephen was about to climb on the bicycle he had rested up against the side of it when Julie tugged him by the shoulder and said, 'Look!' When he turned round he saw to his horror that zombies were coming up the driveway leading to the control-tower. In fact, they were blocking all escape-routes from it.

'We're really fucked this time!' said Stephen, getting his gun out of his rucksack while Julie held her crossbow at the ready. 'Let's go back to the viewing balcony and pick off the zombies from there.'

'No, wait!' said Julie excitedly. 'There's a helicopter over there!'

She manoeuvred him around so that he could see one was beyond a Cessna 172 that had been parked by one of the fuel pumps. It was a single-engine Bell 206L.

'I haven't flown choppers in ages!' he said. 'I told you that last night!'

'I know,' said Julie, 'but it's not something you forget to do. I bet it's just like driving a car.'

'Not quite,' said Stephen. 'It's a bit more complex than that.'

'But there's no way,' said Julie, 'we'll be able to fight off this many zombies. We don't have enough ammunition. It's our only way out of here.'

Stephen knew she was right and not being ready to die just yet he said, 'Okay, let's make a run for it!' He and Julie sprinted across the main runway towards the helicopter and upon reaching it they opened the doors and clambered into it.

Immediately they had strapped themselves into their seats Stephen took a few moments to familiarise himself with the four flight control inputs located in front of him: the cyclic stick similar to a joystick which tilted the rotor disk in a particular direction resulting in the helicopter moving that way, the collective pitch control located on the left side of the pilot's seat which changed the pitch angle of all the main rotor blades at the same time resulting in the helicopter increasing or decreasing in altitude, anti-torque pedals located in the same position as the rudder pedals in a fixed wing aircraft and which controlled the direction in which the nose of the aircraft was pointed; and the throttle which was a motorcycle-style twist grip mounted on the collective control whose purpose was to maintain enough engine power to keep the rotors producing enough lift for flight.

When this was done Stephen suddenly went into automatic pilot flicking numerous switches on the control-panels in front of and above him, whereupon there was a whirring sound as the main and tail rotors began to turn around.

'When can we take off?' said Julie. 'The zombies are closing in on us!'

'In a little while,' said Stephen. 'The rotors must build up momentum first.'

They both shot at the zombies nearest to them who slumped forwards onto the runway before closing the doors each side of the helicopter and then Stephen pulled back on the cyclic and the helicopter lifted into the air and began to hover, which he had always found extremely challenging because it generated its own gusty air which acted against the fuselage and flight control surfaces. This resulted in him making constant control inputs and corrections to keep the chopper where it was meant to be.

When the airspeed had reached approximately 16 knots it provided extra lift whereupon Stephen displaced the cyclic forward which caused the nose of the chopper to pitch down, and then for it to move forward away from the airfield and the zombies at which point he moved the cyclic aft causing the nose to pitch up slowing the helicopter and causing it to climb.

'You did it! You did it!' said Julie ecstatically as they flew over the mass of houses. 'I told you you could!'

'Don't get too excited,' said Stephen checking the fuel-gage. 'We're not out of danger yet. We haven't got a lot of fuel in the tank so we're going to have to look for somewhere to land soon.'

He could not help but smile though that he had managed to conquer his fear of flying albeit under extreme circumstances and Julie was proud of him as a daughter would be proud of a father. The problem now was where to set down the chopper amongst the buildings and Stephen thought they might very well have to land in a road. However he was determined that they should go as far as they could before that became a necessity.

They soon had far more important things to think about though for a zombie, unbeknownst to them, had managed to grab one of the helicopter's skids before they had flown out of the airfield and had now pulled himself up onto it and was standing atop it. All of a sudden he flung the helicopter-door on the passenger side open and made a lunge for Julie who shrieked and tried to fire an arrow from her crossbow at him.

Before she could do so though he had knocked it out of her hand and it dropped down onto the floor in front of her. He then attempted to bite Julie who desperately fought him off.

'Duck Julie! Duck!' said Stephen all of a sudden.

She did as requested and he fired two shots into the zombie's head holding his gun in his right hand while grasping the cyclic in his left one, and watched in relief as it fell backwards and hurtled down to the ground like a rag doll.

'Close the door Julie!' urged Stephen. 'C'mon, you can do it!'

She sat crying her eyes out with her arms folded around her chest in a self-comforting gesture, and it took a lot of coaxing before Stephen was finally able to get her to reach over and pull the door her side shut.

'It's over now,' said Stephen. 'The zombie's gone.'

He looked out of the door his side to make sure there were no more of them clinging to the helicopter's skids and breathed a deep sigh of relief when he saw that there were not. They flew on looking for a landing site for Stephen reckoned they had ten minutes of fuel left and applied pedal inputs in whichever direction was necessary to centre the ball in the *Turn and Bank* indicator. Soon they came upon the motorway whereupon he pushed the cyclic to the right side causing the helicopter to hover sideways. What an odd sensation it was for them to fly above it in a chopper instead of drive along it in a car.

'This is the first time,' laughed Stephen, 'I've ever done anything like this! It wasn't part of my RAF training to fly above motorways!'

Julie smiled as well as they went over several bridges before Stephen spotted a service station up ahead of them.

'We're going,' he said, 'to land by that service station over there. We can stock up with food from the shops there.'

He pointed to where they were going and a few moments later pushed the cyclic to the left before decreasing collective at which point the helicopter descended towards the ground and then landed in the car-park. When it was safely on the ground Stephen flicked a few switches and said, 'Right, be careful Julie when we get out of the helicopter. The rotors'll keep turning for a few more minutes yet so remember to duck.'

She picked her crossbow up off the floor and exited her side of the helicopter and when Stephen had done so his side he was grabbed by a zombie he had not seen. Before he could fire his gun at him he had knocked it out of his hand and there then ensued a desperate struggle as Stephen tried to retrieve it, all the time the helicopter rotors whirring above them.

'Kill the bastard, Julie!' shouted Stephen.

'I can't!' she said in a panic. 'I can't get a clear shot at his head!'

An idea then occurred to Stephen as he continued to wrestle with the zombie and all of a sudden he punched him in the stomach which badly winded him, and then he grabbed hold of him by the waist and lifted him up in the air. The next instant there was a jet of blood from the zombie's neck as his head was severed by the helicopter's rotors, and Stephen was left holding his lifeless body which he threw onto the ground.

He then picked his gun up off it and he and Julie went through the car-park past a petrol station to a large building. Inside it was a self-service restaurant with tables, chairs, plates, knives, forks and rotting bits of food on the floor. There was also a Marks and Spencer's store as well as a WH Smiths, the latter which they entered.

'Hey, look at this Stephen!' said Julie excitedly as she stood in front of a shelf. 'There are loads of bars of chocolate here!'

'Good,' he said. 'Stuff as many as you can in your rucksack and then we'll be off.'

He did the same and they left the service station and wandered through the car-park.

'Where to now?' said Julie munching on a Mars bar.

'I think,' said Stephen, 'we should check out all the cars and see if the zombies have left any keys in their ignitions.'

That is just what they did peering in the windows of the numerous vehicles parked in the car-park without success, and they were just about to give up hope of finding one they could drive when Stephen called out, 'I've found one Julie! Over here!' She immediately rushed over from the Ford Fiesta she had been looking in to Stephen who was standing by a Land Rover.

'This one's,' he said opening the door on the driver's side, 'got keys in the ignition. Get in and then we can get out of here.'

Julie climbed into the passenger-side of the Land Rover and Stephen turned the keys in the ignition and it started first time. Putting it into first gear they pulled out of their parking space and drove round the car-park.

'This car's nearly out of petrol,' said Stephen. 'I'm going to have to put some more in the tank.'

He drove up to the petrol-station, stopped the Land Rover by one of the pumps, switched the engine off and got out of the vehicle. While he was filling up the tank Julie took out a Twix bar from her rucksack and ate it. As soon as the tank was full Stephen got back into the car and he and Julie drove down the slip-road leading into the service station and turned onto the motorway.

CHAPTER SEVEN

What a pleasure it was for Stephen and Julie to be in the only car being driven along the motorway without any traffic to contend with, particularly the tail-gaiters who would stick dangerously to the back of your car sometimes less than a few feet away in an effort to make you go faster, and the people who drove consistently in the third lane even though it was only meant for overtaking. It was also a joy for them to avoid the coaches and heavy lorries that would make your vehicle shudder as they passed by it at excessive speeds.

The only cars Stephen and Julie saw on the motorway were abandoned and crashed ones lying in the middle of it occasionally upturned and with their fronts smashed in. Stephen had to be careful driving around them for shards of glass were on the road which could have easily punctured the Land Rover's tyres.

Where there had been a particularly bad pile-up that was

blocking the three lanes of the motorway he and Julie were travelling along, he would be forced to cross the central reservation (and how he was glad he was driving a Land Rover with four-wheel drive at such times capable of such a manoeuvre) and then travel up the adjacent three lanes the wrong way up the motorway. Not that it mattered seeing as there was no traffic coming from the opposite direction, at least they hoped not, nor any policemen to penalise them for doing so.

Either side of the motorway were hard shoulders bordered by grass verges which gave Julie and Stephen pleasure to look at as did any pieces of greenery which had become so scarce. It induced feelings of tranquillity in them even though they in turn were bordered by row upon row of houses, factories, offices and garages.

London was about seventy miles away and they had enough fuel in the tank to reach it easily, although Stephen did not know what kind of city would greet them when they arrived there. All kinds of thoughts filled his head: would Nelson's Column still be standing? Would the great art treasures in the National Gallery remain intact? Was there any resistance to the zombies? Would the Houses of Parliament ever be the fulcrum of a functioning democracy again?

There were numerous bridges straddling the motorway jam-packed with cars and lorries whose brickwork was crumbling, and Stephen wondered how long it would be before they collapsed completely blocking the motorway.

On both sides if it massive pylons towered above the houses like a succession or morbid Eiffel towers. Living in such close proximity to them had resulted in many people becoming sick and dying. However there was nowhere else to put them and there had always been people willing to move into any abandoned properties near them.

Suddenly Stephen and Julie were roused from their daydreams by the sight of numerous zombies on the road up ahead of them.

'Are you going,' said Julie, 'to cross the central reservation again and drive round them, Stephen?'

'No fucking chance!' he said. 'Watch this!'

He pressed his right foot hard down on the accelerator and Julie clung to the dashboard as the Land Rover smashed into the zombies toppling them like ninepins and sending some flying over the roof. Stephen and Julie watched in the mirrors as they came crashing down the other side of it and then crawled pathetically after them as they were unable to get up as their legs had been broken.

'They fly through the air,' sang Stephen, 'with the greatest of ease, those magnificent men in their flying machines.'

He and Julie then burst out laughing even though they had just killed ten zombies for by now they detested them, and had both developed a black sense of humour as people are wont to do who live and work in stressful and difficult conditions. Thereafter whenever they saw any zombies in the road Stephen would drive directly into them, and then Julie would join him in a verse of Those Magnificent Men in Their Flying Machines. All seemed to be going well and they had made good progress to London, when all of a sudden there was a crashing sound as they approached another bridge.

A zombie who had been standing atop it had dropped a brick onto the windscreen of their Land Rover smashing it and just missing them in the process. Momentarily Stephen's eyes were off the road and on exiting the bridge he swerved to avoid a car going up an embankment. He screamed along with Julie as the Land Rover overturned and rolled back down it to the road where it came to a standstill on its roof.

Stephen and Julie lay there dazed for a little while before he unstrapped himself from his seat, blood streaming from his left ear and a gash in his forehead. Opening the door of the Land Rover his side he crawled out through it and then got to his feet, staggered round to the passenger side and opened the door. Unbuckling a still disorientated Julie from her seat who was covered in cuts and bruises, he pulled her out of the car.

'Julie, are you alright?' he said standing her on her feet and holding on to her for support.

'Er-yes, I think so,' she said groggily. 'What happened?'

'A fucking zombie,' said Stephen going red in the face,

'threw a brick onto the windscreen of our Land Rover, that's what fucking happened! I'm going to fix that bastard right now!'

After getting his and Julie's rucksacks out of the car and putting his one on and then helping her to do the same, they both walked up the embankment, still a little unsteady on their feet, to the top of the bridge they had passed beneath seconds before. The zombie who had thrown the brick at them was walking towards them and Stephen un-holstered his gun and said, 'D'you think that's fucking funny, you throwing a brick on me and a little girl you evil c★★t!'

The zombie just moaned as he continued moving towards Stephen who shot him with a single bullet to the head and watched in satisfaction as he fell backwards.

'Now,' said Stephen, 'that's what I call funny and this!'

He holstered his gun, picked the zombie up, threw him over the side of the bridge and watched as he landed on the concrete below with a thud. Walking back to Julie he put his arm around her and said, 'Let's head for another service station. It'll be dark soon and we can spend the night there.'

They walked back down the embankment and carried on along the motorway past their upturned Land Rover in a dejected state—for the next road sign they saw shortly afterwards informed them that they still had 35 miles to go to reach London and they had a considerable walk ahead of them. However they cheered up when they had travelled a few miles spotting a lone kestrel hovering above the grass verges bordering the motorway in search of rodents, whereupon they saw another sign with *Services:5 Miles* up ahead of them.

'Good,' said Stephen. 'We can make it there before dark.'

That is what they did just as the light was starting to fade and they veered off the motorway along the slip-road leading to the service station reaching it about ten minutes later.

'Tomorrow morning,' said Stephen, 'we can check out all the vehicles in the car-park and see if any still have their keys in the ignition.'

'Okay,' said Julie.

She and Stephen went into the service station where they made for the restaurant, sat down at one of the tables, removed some tins of spaghetti from their rucksacks and opened them.

'Would you like,' said Stephen after they had finished eating, 'me to read you some more of A Little Princess before we go to sleep?'

'Yes,' said Julie who like a lot of children took comfort in the world of fiction where problems, no matter how difficult, were overcome and there was always a happy ending.

CHAPTER EIGHT

Stephen and Julie were awoken the next day in the restaurant of the service station where they had spent the night by a tapping on the window panes caused by a light drizzle. After having a bar of chocolate each for breakfast which they got from the WH Smith store there along with several bags of sweets they made for the Marks and Spencer shop, where they each picked out a new jumper and a pair of jeans discarding their dirty old smelly ones in the process.

With that they left the service station and strolled around the car-park looking for any cars with the keys still in their ignitions without finding any.

'Well, it looks, Julie,' said Stephen, 'that we'll be walking the rest of the way to London unless we can find another car we can use.'

They left the car-park and walked down the road leading from it to the motorway and turned onto it. It stretched for mile upon mile ahead of them like a vast concrete river enclosed by high embankments. It was very tiring on the legs walking along the road exacerbated by the monotony of the urban landscape. At least when the motorway had been surrounded by fields, Stephen thought, it had made travelling along it tolerable.

He was thankful once again to have a companion albeit a little girl, and he wished that maybe one day he could meet another woman who could become a wife to him and a mother to Julie. However, as they went along without sight nor sound of another human being the horrible thought crossed his mind that they might be the last ones left in the whole of Britain.

After about ten miles of travel along the motorway which had no pretension to beauty past an oak tree left in glorious isolation high atop an embankment, Stephen and Julie sighted about five hundred zombies walking towards them.

'Oh shit!' he said. 'There's a whole army of them! I think our motorway journey is at an end for the time being. We can't fight off that many of them.'

'But I thought we were going to London?' said Julie.

'We still are,' said Stephen. 'We'll leave the motorway now and rejoin it at another place.'

Julie perked up on hearing this and Stephen was glad for the last thing he wanted to do was to disappoint her, although he was beginning to doubt that they would now in fact reach London. So they stepped off the motorway onto the embankment, climbed up it and then disappeared amongst the houses that comprised an uninspiring town made up of sprawling suburbs.

'I think,' said Stephen as they went up and down new roads and streets where thousands of semi-detached houses had been built forming a new suburb where previously there had been a village, 'we should stock up on some more food. We're running rather short.'

He had always thought of the suburbs as dull and soulless but the rich variety of houses was rather remarkable. Many were made of the local red brick but rarely without a design in the brickwork and walking along these suburban roads revealed a staggering amount of variation. There were still some doors with brass name plates; windows with coloured and leaded glass; different gables and porches as well as gardens and gates, all refuting the idea that the suburbs are all bland and boring.

Naturally enough many shops and businesses had sprung up to cater for the inhabitants of the new suburbs and it was not long before Stephen and Julie came upon a supermarket. When they had stuffed their rucksacks with as many tinned goods as they could they exited the supermarket and continued with their journey.

The suburb they entered after that had large numbers of terraced houses in varying degrees of size and style together with much grander properties in their own grounds, and within a mile or so of these areas there were a number of shoe and hosiery factories and many other small businesses. It was now one o'clock and Julie said, 'Can we stop and have something to eat now? I'm famished!'

'I don't see why not,' said Stephen. 'We have just stocked up on food after all.'

A bit further on from them were some swimming-baths that had been earmarked for closure to build yet more housing and Stephen said, 'This'll be a good place to stop and have our lunch.' They entered them and headed up some steps to a café overlooking an Olympic-size pool where they sat down at one of the tables and had something to eat.

'I used,' said Stephen, 'to go swimming a lot with my wife and two daughters. They loved splashing about in the water.'

He became silent as he pictured the scene in his mind before he was roused from his day-dream when Julie said, 'Me and my class at school used to go swimming once a week. I've got my fifty metres badge which means I can do one length of the pool.'

All the while they had been talking they had not heard the zombies coming up the steps, about thirty in total, who were now blocking the exit out of the swimming-baths. They did a few minutes later though when there was a groan as the first of the zombies entered the café.

'Shit!' said Stephen. 'It's those bastards again!'

He removed his pistol from his rucksack and shot the first few of them to enter the café but they kept on coming.

'We're going,' he said, 'to have to get out of here, Julie. We don't know how many zombies are coming up the stairs.'

'Yes, but where to?' she said. 'I thought that was the only way out of here.'

'Maybe not!' said Stephen looking round anxiously. 'Follow me!'

He took Julie by the hand and they went over to a door which led out onto seats overlooking the pool where spectators had sat to watch swimming competitions in the pool.

'What's the use in this?' said Julie. 'The zombies are following us here! We're going to be trapped!'

'I don't think so,' said Stephen. 'Throw your rucksack into the pool but first give me your crossbow and all your arrows.'

Julie did as requested and watched as he put them all in a plastic bag along with his gun and its replacement magazines which he tied at the ends to seal it and stop water entering it. He then chucked it in the pool followed by his rucksack and Julie did the same.

'Now what are we going to do?' she said nervously as the zombies closed in on them who were now less than ten feet away.

'Jump!' said Stephen.

'No way!' shrieked Julie who had always been terrified when she had seen people leaping and diving off the ten-metre-high diving-board at her local swimming-baths.

'Look!' said Stephen. 'We're now unarmed! If we don't jump right away the zombies are going to eat bits of us and then we'll become zombies just like them! Take my hand! We'll jump together!'

Julie took hold of the hand he proffered her and they both stood on a couple of the front-row seats and then jumped over the balcony. The next instant they landed in the pool with a loud splash and dropped to the bottom of it, before Stephen helped Julie back up to the surface again and then to swim to the side of the pool where there were some steps.

As soon as she had climbed up them Stephen retrieved their rucksacks and weapons from the middle of the pool before swimming back to the steps and climbing out of it.

'Put your rucksack on!' he said handing Julie her one. 'We're going to get out of here!'

With that they hurried to the main doors leading to the pool with water dripping from their hair and clothes but to their horror they saw more zombies coming through them as well as out of the men's and women's changing-rooms.

'Oh fuck!' shouted Stephen.

'Aargh! We're done for!' screamed Julie.

Frantically Stephen looked around trying to figure out what to do next and in desperation he picked up a nearby chair and threw it against the window to try to break it, but it did not do so as the chair was not heavy enough to shatter the glass only being made of plastic.

'I don't know,' said Stephen, 'how many zombies there are but they're not going to take us without a fight!'

He ushered Julie over to the steps leading up to the ten-metre diving-board and told her to climb up them with him following closely behind. Once at the top of it Stephen removed their weapons from the plastic bag he had put them in and passed Julie's crossbow and arrows to her while he took hold of his gun.

'Right,' he said, 'this is going to be like Custer's Last Stand. We're surrounded on all sides but one thing in our advantage is, unlike the Indians, the zombies are unarmed and can only reach us by climbing up the steps leading to the diving-board but we're going to keep them covered at all times.'

Stephen did not fire at the zombies until they were near to them to increase his chances of killing them for he knew, as did Julie, that it was important not to waste any ammunition at a time like this. Zombie after zombie dropped dead after being shot with their bullets and arrows, some of whom fell into the pool staining it red with their blood and floated face down there.

Stephen made sure he was covering the ladder leading

up to the diving-platform and as soon as a zombie stepped onto it they were shot dead. They kept on coming and the ones on the balcony overlooking the pool began to jump into it driven by their instinct to consume Stephen's and Julie's flesh.

When they had swam over to the side of the pool where the diving-boards were they were picked off by Stephen and Julie though and soon the bodies of ten dead zombies were amassed there, at which point Julie had run out of arrows.

'I've got no more ammunition!' she said.

'No matter,' said Stephen. 'I've got plenty more bullets for those c**ts!'

The zombies kept pouring in to the pool area from all the entrances to it though as well as continuing to jump from the balcony, and Stephen wondered despite his show of defiance whether he and Julie were going to die there of all places. After a while forty zombies were lying dead in and around the pool of all ages, sexes and creeds.

He checked the six remaining magazines which he had spread out on the diving-platform. *That's seventy-eight bullets left*, he thought, *after I've used up the one remaining bullet in the magazine I've got loaded into my gun at the moment.* As Julie was effectively unarmed now he had to cover more ground and moved back and forth along the diving-platform, pausing to fire at zombies as he went. For the last thing he wanted was for a load of them to amass around it and begin to climb up the steps leading to it, potentially increasing the chances of he and Julie being killed when he was forced to reload.

Gradually he got through his remaining magazines until there were only two left and another fifty-two zombies shot through the head. It was a horrific sight with spattered blood, brain matter and skull fragments lying everywhere, so much so that Julie could not help but be sick into the pool over the edge of the diving-platform.

As Stephen loaded yet another magazine into his gun he scoured the pool-area and counted twenty-two zombies. *Good!* he thought. *I've got enough bullets but please don't let there be any more zombies entering the pool-area!* His wish was not met for shortly afterwards another couple of them came into it via the women's changing-room. He still had enough bullets and used them when he was sure he could not miss, shooting dead all the remaining zombies whereupon there were none left in the pool-area.

He and Julie waited anxiously, their hearts pounding in their chests expecting more of them to turn up, first five minutes and then another ten but none did.

'I think we've done it Julie!' sighed Stephen. 'We can climb down from the diving-platform now.'

They did just that all the time listening out for any zombies as they walked round the edge of the pool past the mass of dead ones lying prostrated around it. Stephen managed to pull five of Julie's arrows out of their bodies, grimacing as he handed each of them in turn to her. On reaching the main double doors leading to the pool-area they went through them, then hurried towards the exit and fled from the swimming-baths knowing that their daring exploits there would remain untold in any history books.

CHAPTER NINE

Stephen and Julie walked along roads where former dairies, factories, swimming pools and shops had reached the end of their useful life and had been demolished to be replaced by housing. Stephen had no objection to this or to the many estates which consisted mainly of houses where there were many lush green spaces which he thought worked well. What he did object to was the greatest change to the suburban landscape when the last few farms, allotments and other green spaces were used for building and new roads. At least he thought many important buildings had been saved from destruction and modernisation by a more enlightened attitude and the realisation that the country's heritage needed to be preserved.

The suburbs were not, Stephen realised, as they are often portrayed, rows of identical 1930's semi-detached houses stretching along the arterial routes and major ring roads with more packed in behind them but very diverse areas. However right at that moment he had more pressing concerns, namely that he only had two bullets left in his gun and Julie just had five arrows in her quiver.

'We've got,' said Stephen, 'to get some more ammunition soon. The problem is I'm unfamiliar with this city and don't know where any gun-shops are.'

So they scoured the area for one as they walked along weaving their way between the cars that had crashed into shop-front windows, lampposts, bins and parking-meters. The tall office-blocks and factories stood eerily deserted that had once provided much of the finance for the city, and the Gothic-looking town hall with its tall central steeple had had its walls engulfed by creeping ivy.

They were beginning to give up hope of ever finding a gun-shop when ironically three zombies they saw up ahead of them came to their rescue. For wanting to avoid them as they only had two bullets left they turned down a side-street and walked along it. As they turned a corner both their faces lit up as they came upon a gun-shop that had previously been obscured from view.

'Would you believe it!' said Stephen. 'We've found a gun-shop thanks to those zombies!'

They entered it and found that most of the guns had been looted though as people in the area had fought a desperate battle against the zombies. To Stephen's consternation he was unable to find any replacement magazines for his Browning 9mm but he did spot a single shotgun hanging from a rack on the wall.

'I suppose,' he said lifting it down, 'this'll have to do. It's not what I'm used to handling though.'

He searched around the shop for some cartridges for it, locating a couple of boxes of them in a glass cabinet behind the counter. After loading two into the gun he placed the rest in his pockets before taking out the sole gun left from another cabinet.

'Here, you take this,' he said handing it to Julie. 'It's a Smith and Wesson snub-nosed .38 Special with only a 2" barrel so it should fit into your pocket nicely.'

She aimed it around the shop mouthing the word 'Boom!' as she fired at imaginary zombies.

'Yes, it feels okay to me,' she said.

'It's a hard-kicking gun though,' said Stephen, 'so make sure you grip it tightly with two hands before you fire it at anything. Bullets coming out of the 2" barrel yours has got can suffer velocity and expansion problems. Here, give it to me,' he said searching behind the counter again and bringing up another box from it. 'I'll show you how to load it. I've found some bullets for it.'

Julie watched intently as he pulled out the gun's revolving chamber and placed five bullets in it one by one.

'You've got,' said Stephen counting the spare ones remaining in the box full of them, 'another fifteen bullets left when you've used up the five in your gun. Remember to keep the safety-catch on though like I showed you before until you spot some zombies.'

With that they left the shop, Stephen holding his shotgun having re-holstered his Browning 9mm and Julie clutching her snub-nosed gun. It was starting to get dark by now and the street-lamps lit up automatically illuminating the tall buildings, road-signs and traffic lights around them.

'We'll have to get under cover soon.' said Stephen. 'I don't like being in a built-up area at night. There are too many dark corners and alleyways where zombies can ambush us.'

After they had walked past several shops and cafés and a tower block of flats they sighted a roundabout covered in overgrown bushes, a little oasis of green amongst the brickwork.

'We can set up our tent there,' said Stephen pointing to it.

'Won't that be dangerous,' said Julie, 'with roads all around us?'

'No more than anywhere else.' said Stephen. 'As long as the zombies can't see us we'll be okay.'

They crossed a road to the roundabout where Stephen quickly set about erecting their tent. He had it up in no time at all at which point he left the cover of the bushes and walked around the roundabout making sure he could not see it from the road. When he was satisfied that he could not he stepped back onto the roundabout and disappeared amongst the bushes again.

'It's okay Julie,' he said. 'There's no way any zombies can see us from the road. Let's get into the tent now.'

They did just that and unrolled their sleeping-bags and then Stephen read Julie some more of A Little Princess until he saw her yawn and then her eyes begin to close until she was sound asleep, whereupon he switched off his torch and closed his eyes as well. In the morning the two of them were awoken by the sound of the zipper on their tent being pulled up whereupon a zombie emerged into it with another right behind him. Not having time to reach for his shotgun which was resting on the end of his sleeping-bag, Stephen instead pulled his pistol out of its holster and killed both zombies with the last two bullets in it.

'Evidently,' he said pushing them away from him and Julie and out of the tent, 'this was not such a good place to spend the night.'

They packed up their equipment, left the roundabout and made their way through the city-centre on what once had been a busy commercial stretch of road having a wide variety of specialist shops and restaurants reminding Stephen a little of suburban London. The new suburbs that had to be created to house the ballooning population had swallowed up numerous villages which had been separated from towns and cities by great swathes of open countryside, much to the consternation of the villagers who severely objected to being engulfed by the ever-expanding towns and cities.

As Stephen and Julie went along they occasionally smelt the aroma of perfumed plants coming from gardens much to their delight. They carried on through estates where the council had at least tried to avoid the uniformity that often arose with mass housing by interspersing brick with concrete and using highly coloured roof tiles and different shades of rendering, which were a big improvement on the high-rise blocks of flats built by many local authorities to solve the housing crises in the aftermath of World War Two.

The way now took them past a YWCA centre and a junior school before they turned left and went down a long winding road that led to a golf-course. Climbing a gate Stephen and Julie crossed a patch of rough to a fairway bordering a stream and began to walk along it.

'Ordinarily I hate golf,' said Stephen, 'but boy does it feel good to see so many trees and a stream.'

'Yes, and all the wildlife,' said Julie spotting several grey squirrels darting along tree-branches and even a fallow deer grazing on one of the greens not far off.

A bit further on they came upon an abandoned golf-cart and Stephen said, 'We might as well make use of this.' After putting their rucksacks in the back of it they got onto it and set off along the fairway crossing a green onto another fairway lined by trees. They were just beginning to enjoy themselves when several zombies emerged from the trees and headed their way.

Whenever any of the zombies got too close to them Stephen would stop their cart and he would blast away with his shotgun while Julie fired her gun.

'Ha, I've always,' said Stephen as he and Julie left a trail of dead zombies in their wake, 'felt like shooting people on a golf-course. All those silly visors, checked jumpers, plus-twos and plus-fours they wear and have you seen the damage my shotgun can do! The zombies' heads just come apart!'

On they went, he and Julie, in their golf-cart up and down the fairways and greens stopping every now and then to kill zombies. By the time they had reached the clubhouse the golf-course was littered with the corpses of them.

'That's the best round of golf I've ever played!' laughed Stephen stopping the golf-cart. 'We should have a drink at the nineteenth hole. I've worked up quite a thirst.'

He and Julie stepped off their golf-cart and were about to go into the clubhouse when Julie's eyes opened wide and she pointed up at the sky.

'Wow! Look at that!' she said.

Stephen saw to his amazement a hot-air balloon descending rapidly beneath which was suspended a wicker basket inside of which was a man with long white hair in a flying-jacket and goggles, and then come in to land on the fairway closest to the clubhouse.

'That couldn't be God, could it?' said Stephen as captivated by the sight as Julie was.

He and Julie rushed over to the balloon and the man removed his goggles to reveal a pair of striking turquoise eyes beneath them highlighted by the black marks around them left by the goggles.

'Hello there!' he said. 'I was scanning the area with my binoculars when I saw you two down here and decided to come in to land. The name's Peter Fincham.'

'And I'm Stephen Williams,' said Stephen, 'and this is Julie Mayberry.' He smiled at Julie as he said to Peter, 'Where are you headed?'

'To a country retreat,' said Peter.

'A *country* retreat?' said Stephen incredulously. 'Are there still such places left in Britain?'

Peter stretched his arms and said, 'Yes, at least one that I know of. I take it you two would like to accompany me there?'

'Yes please!' said Julie. 'I've always wanted to fly in a hot-air balloon!'

'That's settled then,' chuckled Stephen.

'Alright,' said Peter. 'Climb aboard.'

Stephen lifted Julie into the balloon's basket and climbed into it himself at which point Peter covered his eyes with his goggles once more, fired the burner several times until the heated air inside the envelope made it buoyant as it had a lower density than the relatively cold air outside the envelope, at which point the balloon began to lift off the ground to Julie's delight. Soon it was high in the air once more and it began to drift over the houses which gradually became smaller and smaller.

As they flew along Peter said, 'It's terrible what's been done to Britain, isn't it? The only green areas left are a few gardens, parks and golf-courses.'

'I agree,' said Stephen, 'but the liberal elite refused to listen to reason and control our population growth. What are you doing anyway flying around in a hot-air balloon?'

'I look for survivors,' said Peter, 'of the zombie invasion to take back to the country retreat I was telling you about. We have a small community of twenty people there and grow our own vegetables on the land and even our own corn to produce wheat to make bread. We also have a few cows, pigs and sheep which provide us with food and clothing.'

'How much land is there,' said Stephen, 'in this retreat of yours?'

'Several acres,' said Peter.

'That much,' said Stephen in astonishment. 'But who did it belong to?'

'You'll see,' said Peter. 'I think you'll be in for a big surprise.'

The balloon travelled at thousands of feet off the ground

and Stephen and Julie felt at peace standing in the basket hanging from beneath it for there was no way any zombies could get to them. The air was still and calm as they floated through white shroud-like clouds feeling extremely safe even though the bottom of the envelope of the balloon was not sealed as the air near it was the same pressure as the surrounding air.

Being so high up in the sky though revealed the true scale of the devastation done to Britain's once beautiful countryside. Where once there had been rolling green fields, glorious woodland and strings of little valleys dotted with farms and houses built from the characteristic local stone, there was now a never ending mass of houses. It induced great feelings of sadness in the three travellers.

'The liberals,' said Stephen breaking the silence, 'got what they wanted in the end but at what a price!'

'Yes,' said Peter. 'They changed Britain for ever.'

After many hours of flight with the wind remaining still and calm and him firing the burner occasionally at the mouth of the balloon he became excited and said, 'We're approaching the country retreat! Can you see it?'

'Yes!' said Julie spotting open parkland dissected by a driveway which spread before a house to the south, all of which was enclosed by a huge twenty-foot-high wall, and to the north was further protected by the rising ground of two hills.

'What's that wall doing there?' said Stephen. 'There's no way your settlement could have built it.'

'No, we didn't,' said Peter. 'We've been very thankful for it though as it has kept out all the zombies. It was built by forces far more powerful than ourselves.'

He made the balloon slowly descend towards the parkland within the wall until they landed gently on it with the basket remaining upright where they were greeted by a group of excited people.

'This is our community,' said Peter clambering out of the basket as did Stephen and Julie and introducing them to the group of smiling men, women and children amassed around the balloon which had begun to deflate.

They began to walk along the driveway until they came to an imposing pair of gates supported by piers which gave access to a walled forecourt and quatrefoil lawn, in the centre of which stood the statue of the Greek goddess Hygeia gracefully upon a plinth. There were two doors in the wall on either side of the forecourt leading to the north lawn and the south garden, and above the latter had been inscribed the exhortation to 'Abandon care'.

Beyond them was a sixteenth-century house of modest proportions built of mellow russet brick with tall chimneys, gables and mullioned windows. On reaching it the front door swung open in welcome as Peter, Stephen and Julie stepped across the threshold into the panelled stone-flagged hall, where there was the smell of wood from the huge fireplace in the Great Hall.

Stephen admired the mellow oak panelling as well as the presence of so many other beautiful things.

'What a wonderful old house this is!' he said. 'There's this incredible feeling of peace and tranquillity here!'

'Yes,' said Peter. 'It was what Lord Lee intended when he bequeathed it to the nation. It nestles inconspicuously in a fold of the Chiltern Hills and is situated about forty miles from London's Downing Street, in a triangle between the Buckinghamshire towns of Great Missenden, Wendover and Princes Risborough. It's called *Chequers*.'

'But that's,' said Stephen, 'the Prime Minister's country residence, isn't it?'

'Yes,' said Peter.

'You mean to say,' said Stephen, 'that he was living here surrounded by countryside while he forced the rest of us to live in urban squalor? The hypocritical bastard!'

He went red in the face with rage as he and Julie were led into the house to see the rest of the sumptuous décor. That night he read Julie the rest of A Little Princess which told of how Sara Crewe was found by chance by Ram Dass, a servant of an intimate friend of her late father called Mr Carrisford. It was he who had brought the wonderful news for Sara that her father's diamond mines which he thought had been worthless, were in fact full of the precious stones and that he would act as her guardian and look after her.

'You see,' said Stephen after he had read the final page

of the book and closed the cover, 'Sara triumphed over all her hardships and found happiness just as I'm sure we both will in our new home.'

Julie smiled as he tucked her up in a bed of her own, the first one she had slept in in ages and in the days and months and years that followed they did find peace and happiness in their country retreat surrounded by the high concrete wall, a microcosm of the great nation Britain had once been.

ND - #0521 - 270225 - C0 - 216/138/7 - PB - 9781909304895 - Matt Lamination